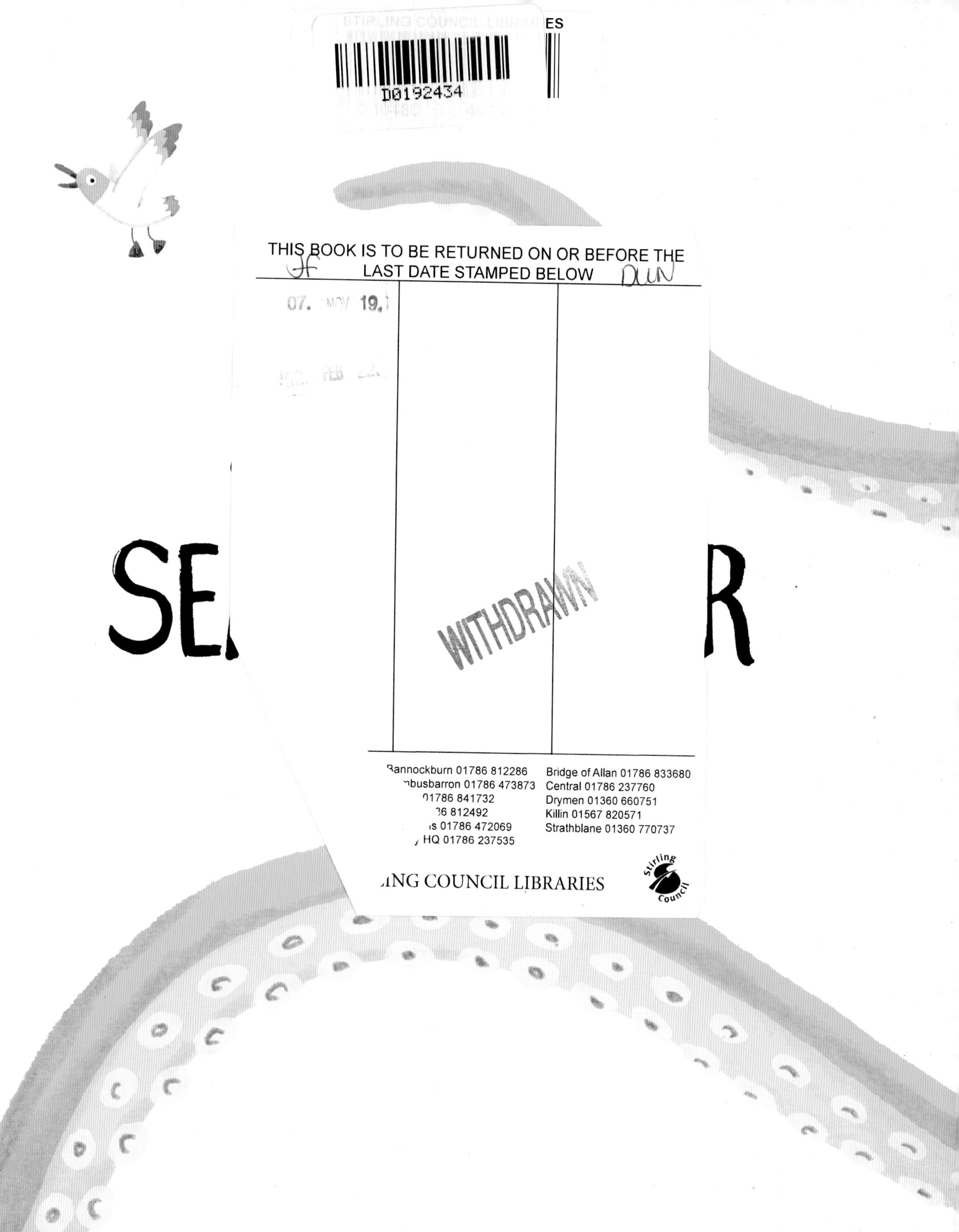
SE
R

OXFORD
UNIVERSITY PRESS

Great Clarendon Street, Oxford OX2 6DP

Oxford University Press is a department of the University of Oxford.
It furthers the University's objective of excellence in research, scholarship,
and education by publishing worldwide. Oxford is a registered trade mark of
Oxford University Press in the UK and in certain other countries

First published 2018

British Library Cataloguing in Publication Data available

ISBN: 978-0-19-275952-8

1 3 5 7 9 10 8 6 4 2

Printed in China

Paper used in the production of this book is a natural, recyclable product made
from wood grown in sustainable forests. The manufacturing process conforms
to the environmental regulations of the country of origin

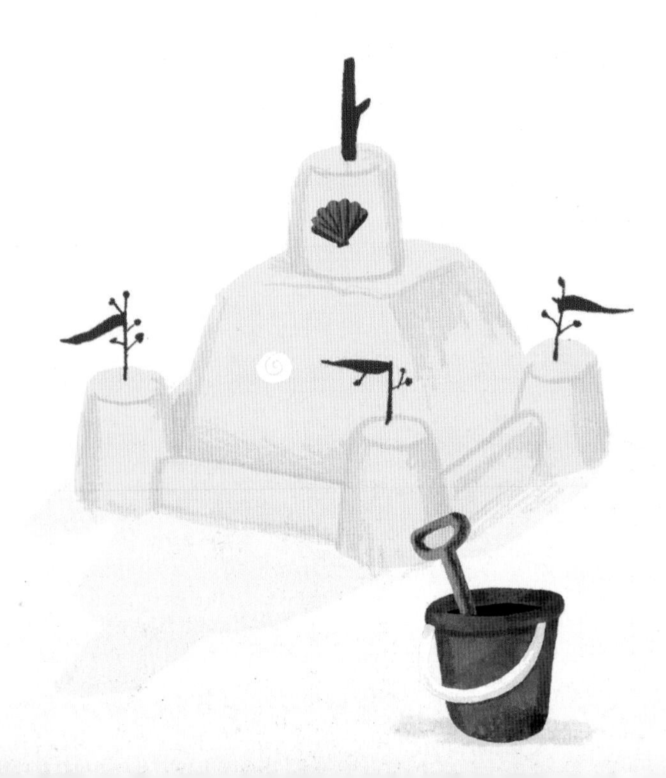

Lula lived in an old house on the beach
with her parents. She loved it there.
But it wasn't going to last much longer.

In a few days time,
she and her family would
have to move out.

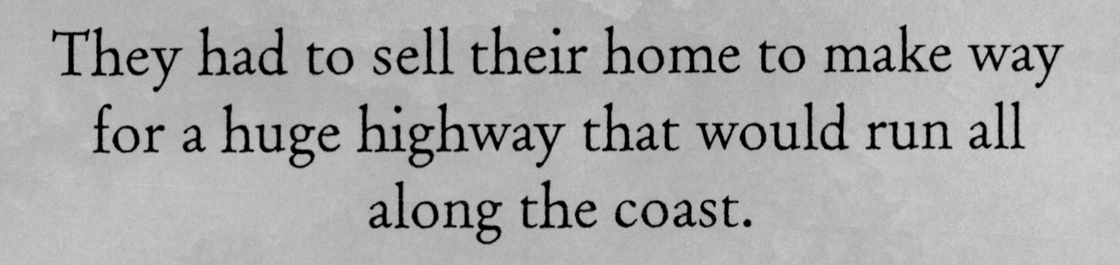

They had to sell their home to make way for a huge highway that would run all along the coast.

Early one morning, Lula packed some sandwiches and took her bucket and spade and went for a walk along the beach.

She loved looking for things that had washed up on the sand. And she spent hours watching the animals that lived in the rock pools.

This morning, she noticed a tiny creature. It was hardly bigger than a bean and a seagull was trying to snap it up in its beak.

Lula chased the gull away.

Then she scooped the scared creature
up in her bucket.

It curled around
Lula's finger and
seemed very happy to
have been rescued.
'Look how teeny-tiny
you are,' said Lula,
'Can I call you
Bean?'

Bean was too small to look after himself in the deep, wide ocean. So Lula searched for a bigger rock pool, with plenty of rocks and crevices to hide from gulls—and set him free there.

'Are you hungry, Bean?' she asked, and without waiting for a reply, she opened her backpack and gave him some of her sandwich.

‘It’s getting late
but I will be back tomorrow,’
Lula told Bean as she walked home.

Lula woke up early the next morning, made three extra sandwiches, and hurried along the beach to see her friend.

But it wasn't a tiny creature she found in the pool. No. Bean had grown overnight and now the pool he was in was too small.

Lula scooped him up in her bucket, though he hardly fitted . . .

. . . and dragged him to a larger pool.

Then she gave Bean all of the sandwiches she'd brought —even her own. And they played until sunset.

The next day Lula packed everything she could carry from the kitchen pantry.

She stuffed it all in a bed sheet and dragged it along the shore.

And she found that Bean had grown even

bigger!

So Lula used the food she'd brought to
lure him to an extra large rock pool.

And then she fed
him all of the things
she'd brought.
He ate everything!

But as much as Lula loved
Bean, she began to feel
a terrible sadness . . .

Finally it was moving day and with it came the roar of bulldozers. Lula watched her mum and dad pack the last of their belongings into their car. They looked as sad as she felt.

'Lula,' they called, 'it's time for us to go.'
But Lula wouldn't go. She couldn't. This was their home!
And not just theirs! This stretch of beach was home to
millions of little creatures far smaller than she was.

So she marched down and stood in front of the bulldozers.
'I'm not going anywhere!' she shouted.
The men in their bulldozers laughed.

'I mean it!' Lula yelled.
But the bulldozers crept forward,
puffing black smoke into the air.

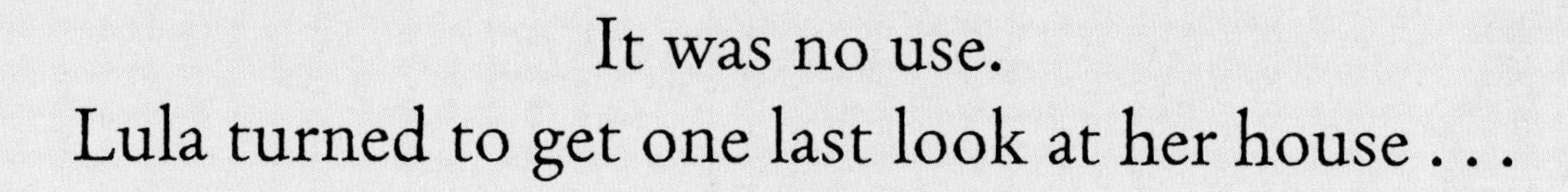

It was no use.
Lula turned to get one last look at her house . . .

And do you know what she saw?

She saw her friend,
bigger now than ten
elephants, curled
around her home—the
way he'd curled around
her finger the first day
they'd met.

Quite suddenly, the men in their bulldozers stopped laughing and turned round and raced away.

Lula still lives in her house with her parents.
And there is no highway on the beach.

Of course the
bulldozers came back,
three more times
actually,

but each time Bean
chased them away.

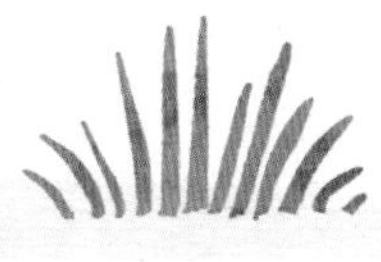

Lula walks along the sand every day, looking for interesting things and animals that need looking after. And most days, Bean swims along in the shallows.

And they couldn't be happier.